Enid Blyton

THE SECRET SEVEN

ADVENTURE ON THE WAY HOME

Enid Blyton

THE SECRET SEVEN

ADVENTURE ON THE WAY HOME

Illustrated by Tony Ross

Hodder
Children's
Books

THE SECRET SEVEN

PETER JANET JACK COLIN

GEORGE PAM BARBARA

Have you read them all?

… now try the full-length **SECRET SEVEN** mysteries:

THE SECRET SEVEN

SECRET SEVEN ADVENTURE

WELL DONE, SECRET SEVEN

SECRET SEVEN ON THE TRAIL

GO AHEAD, SECRET SEVEN

GOOD WORK, SECRET SEVEN

SECRET SEVEN WIN THROUGH

THREE CHEERS, SECRET SEVEN

SECRET SEVEN MYSTERY

PUZZLE FOR THE SECRET SEVEN

SECRET SEVEN FIREWORKS

GOOD OLD SECRET SEVEN

SHOCK FOR THE SECRET SEVEN

LOOK OUT, SECRET SEVEN

FUN FOR THE SECRET SEVEN

SCAMPER

ISBN 978-1-444-92764-1

CHAPTER ONE

'Well, it's about time to go home,' said Peter, looking at his watch. 'I've still got some homework to do, too, worse luck. Come on, Janet.

Thanks awfully for a jolly nice time, Colin.'

'Nice to have you all!' said Colin, as Peter and Janet and the rest of the Secret Seven went to the door. He had asked them all to tea on a dark winter's afternoon, and they had played card games and a mad game of tiddlywinks, and had a jigsaw competition, which Janet won easily.

'Oooh – isn't it dark?' said Barbara, as they all stood on the front door step. 'Not even a star to be seen. Anyone brought a torch?'

The boys had torches, and flashed them on as they walked down to the front gate. Colin shouted a last goodbye and shut the door. Scamper, the golden spaniel, ran ahead – he was always asked out to

tea when the others were, of
course.

The six children walked
down the road and round the
corner.

'Let's take the short-cut
down by the canal,' said Peter.

'Then we can leave George at his house on the way.'

'I don't like that cut by the canal,' said Pam. 'It's so dark. Anything might happen!'

'Let it!' said Jack. 'Who minds if something happens! It would be fun. I wouldn't mind a spot of adventure this evening. I feel excited after all those games.'

'Well, adventures never

come if you expect them,' said Janet, and walked straight into a dustbin that someone had left outside a door.

Crash!

Janet yelled and three torches were shone on her at once. Jack picked up the dustbin lid, which Janet had knocked off, and Peter looked to see

if his sister had hurt herself. She rubbed her right knee and groaned.

'I might have known that something silly would happen if I said that about adventures!' she said. 'Oooh, my knee! Why ever do people leave dustbins on the pavement?'

As they stood there, waiting for Janet to stop groaning, Scamper suddenly gave a **growl**. Peter shone his torch on to him.

'What's up, Scamper? Did the falling dustbin frighten you?'

Scamper was staring across the road, standing perfectly stiff, his tail down. The children looked across the road, too. What was Scamper so interested in?

A row of tall houses used

for offices and small factories stood dark and silent in the cold winter's evening. Only one window showed a light, and that was not very bright because a ragged blind was pulled down over it. The light shone through the gaps in the blind.

As the six stood there, they heard a scream and a little cold shiver of fright

ran over them. Scamper
growled again, and the hair
rose at the back of his neck,
just as it did when he saw a
dog he didn't like.

'Something's up,' said
Peter uneasily. 'What shall
we do? Listen – now there's
somebody shouting!'

They all listened intently,
their eyes fixed on the lit
window with the torn blind.

A shadow suddenly passed
across it, and Janet clutched
Pam.

'Look! That was a man's
shadow – and he had his
hand up – he was going to hit
someone. Oh, there's another

scream. Peter, what shall we do?'

'I'll go and tell Colin – he ought to be in on this,' said Jack. 'I'll bring a rope, too. One of us can climb up to that window and see what's going on. I won't be a minute!'

CHAPTER THREE

In great excitement Jack shot
off, back to Colin's house.
Peter put his hand on the
growling Scamper. 'Let's go
and try the door of that

house,' he said. 'It might be unlocked, you never know. It would be much easier to go in and up the stairs than to mess about with a rope.'

They crossed the road cautiously, switching off their torches. They came to a few steps that ran up to the front door of the house, and Peter went up to the door itself.

He found a handle there and turned it. But the door would not open. As he had expected, it was locked. He felt about for the letterbox, pushed it open and looked through it, flashing his torch there at the same time. But all he could see was a dark, rather dusty-looking hall, with boxes piled high on one side. The house was obviously used as offices and probably was a warehouse, too.

'Nothing to be seen,' said Peter, switching off his torch. 'My word – something *is* certainly going on up there. There was a most bloodcurdling **howl** just then!'

The five children on the doorstep felt most uncomfortable, and Barbara was scared. The **shouts** and

cries sounded so fierce and the **screams** so helpless – and there were now loud **thuds**, too.

Whatever *was* going on? 'I'm going for the police,' said Peter, making up his mind.

CHAPTER FOUR

'You girls had better come with me. George, you stay here with Scamper.'

But Scamper would not stay with George. He wanted

to go with Peter and Janet, of course. So, in the end, Peter ran off alone to get the police, and George and the three girls were left with Scamper to guard them.

Just round the corner Peter bumped into two running boys – Colin and Jack.

Colin, very excited, carried his mother's clothes-line, as that was the only rope

he could think of. He clutched
at Peter, recognising him
by the rather dim light of a
nearby lamppost.

'What's up, Peter? What's
happened now? Why are you
running away?' demanded
Jack.

'I'm fetching the police,'
said Peter. 'Something jolly
serious is going on – and
somebody's being hurt!'

He dashed off, and Colin and Jack ran to join the girls and George.

'Hello!' he panted. 'I've brought a rope. Now we'll be able to see what's happening!'

They shone their torches upwards, and Jack pointed to a signboard swinging just below the lit window.

'Throw the rope over the iron arm that holds the sign,'

he said. 'Here – tie a stone to one end, and hurl it up. Then one of us can shin up easily.'

They tied a stone to the rope end, and then Colin

threw it deftly up to the
signboard that was swinging
in the wind. It fell neatly over
it, and the heavy stone brought
the other end of the rope
down to the waiting children.

CHAPTER FIVE

'Good – now we've got a
double rope to climb,' said
Colin, pleased.

He knotted the two ends
together and twisted the

double strands so that Jack
would have a good hold as he
climbed up.

'There you are,' he said.
'Now you can shin up the
rope just as you do at gym! I'll
hold it steady so that it doesn't
untwist.'

'Hurry up, for goodness'
sake!' said Pam, as another yell
came from the room above.
'I can't bear this much longer!'

Jack shinned up the rope. He came to the signboard jutting out from the brick wall under the lit-up window and pulled himself up by it to the strong iron bar that held it. Cautiously he first sat, then stood on the bar, and found himself waist high with the window ledge. He sat on the ledge and peered through a tear in the blind. What he saw

made him slide down the rope
at top speed, almost tearing
his hands as he went.

'What is it? What did
you see?' asked the others,
crowding round.

'**Whew**!' said Jack,
rubbing his hands gently. 'It's a
good thing Peter's gone for the
police. There are about nine
people there, all going mad,
as far as I can see. They've got

awful faces, and they're yelling at one another and they've got knives, and two of them are lying on the floor, and a poor girl is kneeling down, crying for mercy, and . . .'

'My word!' said Colin, shocked, and the others gasped in horror, too. Scamper growled again and again, and then gave such an ENORMOUS **growl** that he made the children jump. They heard the sound of running feet, and held their breath.

Who was this coming at top speed?

CHAPTER SIX

Ah – thank goodness, it was Peter and two burly policemen. Everyone heaved sighs of relief. Peter ran up, panting.

'Anything else happened?

Quick, tell me!'

'I climbed up to that signboard and peeped in at the window through a hole in the blind,' said Jack. 'There's a **terrible quarrel** going on, and . . .'

The policemen listened as Jack gabbled out what he had seen. All was quiet in the room above now – not a shout was to be heard, not a scream, not a thud. Had the people there heard the arrival of the police?

'We'll go in,' said one of the policemen. 'Look, this bottom window's not fastened. Give me a leg-up, Joe.'

Both men went in – and, of course, the Secret Seven at once followed. They were not going to be left out of the fun! Besides, everyone felt quite

differently now that they had
two stout, burly policemen
with them! Scamper was
left outside, and **whined**
miserably.

Everyone crossed the
office in which they found
themselves, and went into
the hall and up the stairs.
The policemen had rubber-
soled shoes and went quietly.
The Seven, following some

way behind – in case the two policemen saw them and sent them back – went quietly, too, their hearts beating fast.

Really, what a very sudden adventure.

CHAPTER SEVEN

The police came to a door,
under which a crack of light
showed. They stood and
listened. The Seven came
cautiously along, too, and

stood on the landing, hoping that the policemen would not see them in the darkness.

A voice came sharply from inside the room. 'Now then – up you get! That's enough rest. Where's my knife? **Scream**, Margaret, and you, Hal, **yell** at her.'

Then the screaming and shouting began again, with pants and thuds. It seemed as if a terrific fight had begun all over again. The children clutched one another in fright.

One of the policemen flung open the door, and at once bright light streamed on to the landing. 'Now then – what's all this? What's going on here?' said the first policeman, standing in the doorway, gazing at the

strange, startled faces turned towards him.

'Well! I *like* that! What are *you* doing here, I should like to know?' said a man's voice angrily. Peter saw that he held a knife in his hand. 'We've got permission to use this room – you ask the owner of this warehouse. We all work here.'

'Maybe. But what's all

this fighting and quarrelling – and just you put that knife down, young man,' said the policeman, taking out a notebook and pencil.

A girl came forward with brilliant red cheeks, eyes made up in green and black, and an untidy mop of red hair which looked like a wig. She laughed.

'Did you think this was a *real* quarrel, a *real* fight?'

she said. 'It's not! We're
rehearsing a pirate play, and
this is the fight scene, where
I'm captured and a fight goes
on between the pirates and

my rescuers. I have to scream like anything! We're giving the play tomorrow, that's why we're all dressed up and our faces are made up with grease-paint!'

The two policemen were quite taken aback, and went off with many apologies.

The Secret Seven scuttled downstairs in dismay. Goodness gracious! So it was just the rehearsal of an exciting play. *Now* they would get into trouble for fetching two policemen along for nothing!

CHAPTER EIGHT

But they didn't get into trouble.
The policemen were very nice
indeed about the whole thing.
'You did right to fetch us,'
said one. 'It *might* have been

something serious. You couldn't possibly tell. Now, you run home before you find any more adventures – or your next one will be your parents after you!'

Peter told his father and mother why he and Janet and Scamper were so late. They had been very anxious about them. Peter's father laughed when he heard of the evening's happenings.

'Well, well, you're always wanting to put your noses into something! Shall I get tickets for the pirate show tomorrow evening – and take all the Secret Seven with me?'

'Oh, *yes!*' said Peter in delight. 'What a lovely end to an adventure that wasn't really an adventure. But, my word – it did *seem* like one, didn't it, Janet?'

'It did,' said Janet. 'But now everything's all right, and let's hope that *none* of the Secret Seven gets into a row.'

Nobody did except Colin – he had left his mother's clothes-line hanging over the swinging signboard! His mother won't let him go to the pirate play unless he fetches it back. It's all right, Colin – it's still there!